A WOMAN'S STORY

Annie Ernaux
<small>TRANSLATED BY</small> Tanya Leslie

SEVEN STORIES PRESS

NEW YORK | OAKLAND | LONDON

Seven Stories Press
140 Watts Street
New York, NY 10013
http://www.sevenstories.com/

Library of Congress Cataloging-in-Publication Data
    Ernaux, Annie, 1940–
        [Femme. English]
        A woman's story / Annie Ernaux ; translated by Tanya Leslie
        p. cm.
        ISBN 1-58322-575-7 (Trade pbk.)
        1. Ernaux, Annie, 1940– —Family. 2. Authors, French—20th century—
    Family relationships. 3. Mothers—France—Biography. 4. Alzheimer's
disease. I. Title.

PQ2665.R67Z464213 2003
843'.914—dc21   2003009351

College professors and high school and middle school teachers
may order free examination copies of Seven Stories Press titles.
Visit https://www.sevenstories.com/pg/resources-academics
or email academics@sevenstories.com.

Printed in the USA.

9 8 7 6

A WOMAN'S STORY

A WOMAN'S STORY

It is said that contradiction is unthinkable; but the fact is that in the
pain of a living being it is even an
actual existence.

—HEGEL

MY MOTHER DIED on Monday 7 April in the old people's home attached to the hospital at Pontoise, where I had installed her two years previously. The nurse said over the phone: "Your mother passed away this morning, after breakfast." It was around ten o'clock.

For the first time the door of her room was closed. The body had already been washed and a strip of gauze had been wrapped around her head and under her chin,

I

pushing all the skin up around her eyes and mouth. A sheet covered her body up to her shoulders, hiding her hands. She looked like a small mummy. The cot sides had been taken down and left on either side of the bed. I wanted to slip her into the white nightdress with a crochet border that she had once bought for her own funeral. The nurse told me one of the staff would see to this and would also take the crucifix my mother kept in her bedside drawer and place it on her chest. The two screws that pinned the copper arms on to the cross were missing. The nurse wasn't sure they could be replaced. It didn't matter, I wanted her to have her crucifix all the same. On the trolley stood the bunch of forsythia I had brought the day before. The nurse suggested I go straight to the administration office while they drew up an inventory of my mother's personal belongings. She had very few things of her own left—a suit, a pair of blue summer shoes, an electric shaver.

At the administration office, a young woman asked me what I wanted. "My mother died this morning." "Was she registered at the hospital or as a long-term patient? What was her name?" She consulted a sheet of paper and gave a faint smile: she had already been informed. She went and fetched my mother's record and asked a few questions about her, where she was born, her last address before being admitted as a long-term patient. These details were probably in the file.

In my mother's room, a plastic bag with her belongings had been set aside on the bedside table. The nurse asked me to sign the inventory. I decided not to keep the clothes and other possessions she'd had at the hospital. All I took was a small Savoyard chimney sweep from Annecy and a statuette she and my father had bought when they made the pilgrimage to Lisieux. Now that I was there, my mother could be taken to the hospital morgue (it was customary for the body of the deceased to remain in its room for a period of two hours following the time of death). As I was leaving, I caught sight of the woman who shared my mother's room. She was sitting in the sister's office, behind the glass partition, with her handbag in her lap. She had been asked to wait there until my mother's body was moved to the morgue.

My ex-husband went with me to the undertaker's. Behind the wreaths of artificial flowers, a few armchairs were arranged around a coffee table with some magazines. An assistant took us into a room and asked us questions about when she had died, where the burial was to take place and whether or not we wanted a service. He wrote everything down on an order form, occasionally jabbing at a pocket calculator. Then he led us into a dark room with no windows and switched on the light. A dozen coffins were standing against the wall. The assistant explained: "All our prices include tax." Three of the coffins were open so that customers could also choose the color of the lining. I settled for oak because it had been her favorite tree and because she had always wanted to know whether the furniture she bought was made of oak. My ex-husband suggested mauve for the lining. He was proud, almost happy to remember that she often wore blouses of the same color. I wrote out a check for the assistant. The firm took care of everything, except the supplying of flowers. I got home around midday and had a glass of port with my ex-husband. My head and my stomach started to ache.

Around five o'clock I called the hospital to ask if I could go and see my mother at the morgue with my two sons. The girl on the switchboard told me it was too late, the morgue closed at half past four. I got out the car and drove around the new part of town near the hospital, trying to find a flower shop open on a Monday. I asked for white lilies but the florist advised against them: they were suitable only for children, possibly for young girls.

The burial took place on the following Wednesday. I arrived at the hospital with my two sons and my ex-husband. The morgue wasn't signposted and we lost our way before discovering the low, concrete building which lay on the edge of the fields. An assistant in a white coat was talking on the phone. He signaled to us to sit down in a corridor. We sat on chairs lined up against the wall, opposite the lavatories. Someone had left the door open. I wanted to see my mother once more and place on her breast the two twigs of japonica blossom I had brought with me. We didn't know whether they intended to show us the body one last time before closing the coffin. The undertaker's assistant we had seen in the shop emerged from an adjoining room and graciously asked us to follow him. My mother was lying in the coffin, her head thrown back, her hands clasped together on the crucifix. The white gauze had been removed and she was wearing the nightdress with the crochet border. The satin shroud reached up to her chest. It was in a large, bare room with concrete walls. I don't know where the faint light came from.

The assistant informed us that the visit was over and he led us back into the corridor. I felt that he had shown us my mother simply to prove that his firm had carried out its duties satisfactorily. We drove through the new part of town until we reached the church, which had been built next to the arts center. The hearse hadn't arrived so we waited in front of the church. Across the street, someone with tar had smeared "Money, consumer goods, and the State are the three pillars of apartheid" on the façade of the supermarket. A priest stepped forward. He addressed me in affable tones— "Was she your mother?"—and asked my sons where they went to university and what they were studying.

A curious little empty bed, edged with red velvet, had been laid down on the bare cement floor in front of the altar. Later on, the undertakers placed my mother's coffin on top of it. The priest switched on a tape recorder that played organ music. We were the only people present at the service, nobody around here knew my mother. The priest sang canticles and spoke of "eternal life" and "the resurrection of our sister." I wanted the ceremony to last forever, I wanted more to be done for my mother, more songs, more rituals. The organ music started up again and the priest extinguished the candles on either side of the coffin.

Immediately after the service, the undertaker's hearse left for Yvetot, in Normandy, where my mother was to be buried beside my father. I traveled in my own car with my sons. It rained during the whole journey, with the wind blowing in sharp gusts outside. The boys questioned me about the service because it was their first experience and they hadn't known how to behave during the ceremony.

In Yvetot, the family had assembled near the entrance to the cemetery. One of my cousins shouted to me from a distance, "What weather! You'd think we were in November," to cover the embarrassment of watching us approach. We all walked together towards my father's grave. It lay open, the freshly dug earth forming a yellow mound on one side. My mother's coffin was brought forward. When it was lowered into the pit, the men holding the ropes told me to step forward so that I could see it slide down in the hole. A few meters away, the gravedigger was waiting with his spade. He had a ruddy complexion and was wearing blue overalls, a beret, and boots. I felt like going up to him and giving him a hundred francs, thinking he might want to spend it on drinking. There was no harm in that. After all, he would be the last man to take care of my mother, by covering her with earth all afternoon, he might as well enjoy it.

The family insisted that I eat something before I left. My mother's sister had arranged for us to have lunch at a restaurant after the funeral. I decided to stay, I felt this was something I could still do for my mother. The service was slow, we talked about our work and the children. Occasionally we mentioned my mother. They said to me, "What was the point of her going on like that." They all thought it was a good thing she had died. The absolute certainty of this statement is something I cannot understand. I drove back home in the evening. Everything was definitely over.

THE WEEK following the funeral, I would start to cry for no particular reason. As soon as I awoke, I knew my mother was dead. I emerged from a heavy slumber, remembering nothing of my dreams except that my mother was in them, dead. All I did were the daily chores necessary for living: shopping, cooking, loading the washing machine. Quite often I forgot how to do things in the right order. After peeling vegetables, I would have to stop and think before going on to the next stage, that is, washing them. To read was simply impossible. One day I went down to the cellar and

9

there was my mother's suitcase. In it were her purse, a summer handbag, and some scarves. I stood paralyzed in front of the gaping suitcase. The worst moments were when I left home and drove into town. I would be sitting behind the wheel and suddenly it would hit me: "She will never be alive anywhere in the world again." I couldn't come to terms with the fact that the other people behaved normally. The meticulous care with which they chose their meat at the butcher's filled me with horror.

This condition is gradually easing. Even so, I still feel comforted by the fact that the weather is cold and wet, as in the first days of the month, when my mother was alive. I still get that sinking feeling every time I realize "now I don't need to" or "I no longer have to" do this or that for her. I feel such emptiness at the thought: this is the first spring she will never see. (Now I can feel the power of ordinary sentences, or even clichés.)

Tomorrow, it will be three weeks since the funeral. It was only the day before yesterday that I overcame the fear of writing "My mother died" on a blank sheet of paper, not as the first line of a letter but as the opening of a book. I could even bring myself to look at some of her photographs. One of them shows her sitting on the banks of the Seine, her legs tucked neatly beneath her. It's a black-and-white photograph but I can clearly see her flaming red hair and the sun reflected in her black alpaca suit.

I shall continue to write about my mother. She is the only woman who really meant something to me and she had been suffering from senile dementia for two years. Perhaps I should wait until her illness and death have merged into the past, like other events in my life— my father's death and the breakup with my husband— so that I feel the detachment which makes it easier to analyze one's memories. But right now I am incapable of doing anything else.

It's a difficult undertaking. For me, my mother has no history. She has always been there. When I speak of her, my first impulse is to "freeze" her in a series of images unrelated to time—"she had a violent temper," "she was intense in everything she did"—and to recall random scenes in which she was present. This brings back only the fantasy woman, the one who has recently appeared in my dreams, alive once more, drifting ageless through a tense world reminiscent of psychological thrillers. I would also like to capture the real woman, the one who existed independently from me, born on the outskirts of a small Normandy town, and who died in the geriatric ward of a hospital in the suburbs of Paris. The more objective aspect of my writing will probably involve a cross between family history and sociology, reality and fiction. This book can be seen as a literary venture as its purpose is to find out the truth about my mother, a truth that can be conveyed only by words. (Neither photographs, nor my own memories, nor even the reminiscences of my family can bring me this truth.) And yet, in a sense, I would like to remain a cut below literature.

Yvetot is a cold town, situated on a windswept plateau lying between Rouen and Le Havre. At the turn of the century, it was an important administrative center and the trading capital of a region entirely dependent on farming, controlled by a group of wealthy landowners. My grandfather, who worked as a carter on one of the local farms, and my grandmother, who earned a living from cottage weaving, moved to Yvetot a few years after they were married. Both came from a village three kilometers away. They rented a small cottage with a courtyard in a rural area on the outskirts of town. They were located beyond the railway, somewhere between the last cafés near the station and the first fields of colza. It was there that my mother was born in 1906, the fourth in a family of six. She prided herself on telling people: "I wasn't born in the country."

Four of the children never left the town at all and my mother spent three-quarters of her life in Yvetot. They moved closer to the town center but never actually lived there. They would "go into town" to attend mass, to buy meat, and to send postal orders. One of my cousins now has a flat in the town center, cut across by the N15, a main road streaming with lorries night and day. She gives her cat sleeping pills to stop it from going out and getting run over. The area where my mother spent her childhood is very much sought-after by people with high incomes because of its quiet atmosphere and old buildings.

My grandmother laid down the law and made sure her children were taught their place, shouting at them and hitting them when necessary. She was an energetic worker, and a difficult person to get on with. Reading serials was her only relaxation. She had a gift for writing and came top in her *canton* when she passed her primary certificate. She could have become a schoolmistress but her parents wouldn't let her leave the village. Parting with one's family was invariably seen as a sign of misfortune. (In Norman French, "ambition" refers to the trauma of separation; a dog, for instance, can die of ambition.) To understand this story—which ended when she turned eleven—one must remember all those sentences beginning with "in the old days": In the old days, one didn't go to school like today, one listened to one's parents, and so on.

She was a good housekeeper, in other words, she managed to feed and clothe her family on practically no money at all. When the children lined up in church, they were dressed decently (no holes or stains), approaching a state of dignity which allowed the family to live without feeling like paupers. She turned back the collars and cuffs of the boys' shirts so that they would last twice as long. She kept everything, stale bread, the skin off the milk for making cakes, ashes for doing the laundry, the dying heat of the stove for drying plums and dishcloths, and the water used for our morning wash so that we could rinse our hands during the day. She knew all the household tips that lessened the strain of poverty. This knowledge—handed down from mother to daughter for many centuries—stops at my generation. I am only the archivist.

My grandfather, a strong, gentle man, died of a heart attack at the age of fifty. My mother was thirteen at the time and she adored him. After he died, my grandmother's attitude hardened and she became suspicious of everyone. (She was haunted by visions of horror—going to prison, for boys, and having an illegitimate child, for girls.) When cottage weaving died out, she took in people's laundry and cleaned offices.

Towards the end of her life, she moved in with the youngest daughter and her husband. They lived down by the railway, in a prefab without electricity which was once used as a refectory for the factory next door. My mother took me to see her on Sundays. She was a small, plump woman, remarkably agile despite being born with one leg shorter than the other. She read novels, spoke little, and was brusque in her manner. She enjoyed drinking eau-de-vie, which she mixed with the coffee dregs in the bottom of her cup. She died in 1952.

My mother's childhood, in a nutshell:
- an insatiable appetite. She wolfed down the makeweight on her way back from the baker's. "Until I was twenty-five, I could have devoured the whole sea, and all the fish with it!"
- the six children packed into one room, sharing a bed with one of her sisters, the bouts of sleepwalking, when she was found standing in the courtyard, sound asleep, her eyes wide open . . .
- the dresses and pairs of shoes handed down from one sister to the next, a rag doll for Christmas, the apple cider that ruined one's teeth.
On the other hand:
- going for rides on the old carthorse, skating on the

frozen pond in the winter of 1916, skipping games and hide-and-seek, and the insults thrown at the "young ladies" who went to the local convent school (these insults were accompanied by the ritual sign of contempt—turning around and slapping one's bottom sharply);

– leading the full outdoor life of a little country girl, displaying the same knowledge as the boys: sawing wood, shaking the fruit off apple trees, and killing hens by plunging a pair of scissors down their throat. There was, however, one difference: she made sure no one touched her "place."

She went to the local primary school, missing class when she was needed in the fields or when one of her brother or sisters fell ill. She remembered little of this period, only that the schoolmistresses expected the girls to be polite and clean: they inspected their collars and fingernails and asked them to remove one of their shoes (they never knew which foot to wash). My mother went through school without experiencing the slightest flicker of enthusiasm. In those days, nobody "pushed" their children, they had to "have it in them."

School was merely a phase one went through before earning a living. One could miss school, it wasn't the end of the world. But not mass. Even if one stood at the back of the church, one could share in the beauty, the opulence, and the spirit of the ceremony—gold chalices, embroidered chasubles, hymns—and get the impression one didn't live in total poverty. Early in life, my mother developed a strong taste for religion. Catechism was the one subject she learned with passion and she knew all the answers by heart. (Later, in church, her responses were said in the same breathless, exalted tones, as if to show that she knew.)

She was neither happy nor unhappy to leave school at the age of twelve-and a half, the common practice in

† It would be a mistake to speak only in the past. In an article published by the French newspaper Le Monde, dated 17 June 1986, the Haute-Normandie, where my mother was brought up, is subjected to severe criticism: "Despite recent improvements, this region is still suffering from appallingly low schooling standards. . . . Every year the French educational system turns out 7,000 unskilled school-leavers. These young people come straight from 'remedial classes' and therefore do not qualify for training courses. According to an academic expert, half of them 'are unable to understand even two pages written to their standard.'"

those days.[†] She got herself a job in a margarine factory where she suffered from the cold and the damp, her wet hands developing chilblains that stayed with her all winter. After that, she couldn't stand the sight of margarine. So, no "dreamy adolescence" for her, but the long wait until Saturday evening and the pay one brought back to one's mother, saving just enough to afford some face powder, a copy of *L'Echo de la Mode*,[†] and a few giggles and grudges. One day the foreman got his scarf caught in one of the machines. Nobody came to his rescue and he had to disengage himself on his own. My mother was standing right next to him. How can one understand her attitude without having been subjected to the same degree of alienation?

In the wake of the industrialization of the twenties, a

† Probably the most popular women's weekly in France between the two world wars. Originally launched in 1880 as *Le Petit Journal de la Mode*, subsequently renamed *Le Petit Echo de la Mode* and later known as *L'Echo de la Mode*, this Sunday magazine covered a wide range of topics, including fashion, dressmaking, knitting, cooking, and gardening. It also provided invaluable household tips, as well as advice on childcare and medical matters. Last but not least, it published feature stories and romantic fiction (the serials could also be bought separately, in bound volumes). It closed down in 1955.

rope factory was set up in the area, tapping all the local youth. My mother was taken on, as were her sisters and two brothers. To make life easier, my grandmother moved into a small house a hundred meters away from the factory, where she and her daughters did the cleaning after work. My mother liked it in the clean, dry workshops, where one was allowed to chat and joke. She was proud of her job. Working in a big factory made her feel civilized compared to the barbarians—the country girls who stayed behind with the cows—and free compared to the slaves—the housemaids reduced to "licking the arses of the rich." And yet she realized how removed she was from her one and only dream: to become a shop girl.

Like many large families, my mother's family was a tribe: my grandmother and her children had the same way of behaving in public and of living out their semi-rural working condition. This meant that people knew at once who they were, "the D—s." Whatever the circumstances, they would always be shouting, both the men and the women. Despite their gay, exuberant nature, they were touchy and quick to take offense, telling people straight out what they thought of them. Above all, they were proud of the effort they put into their work. They found it hard to believe that anyone could show greater physical commitment. They overcame the limitations of their class by assuming they were "somebody." This may explain the frenzy with which they consumed everything, their work, their food, laughing hysterically, only to announce an hour later, "I'm going to drown myself in the water tank."

My mother was the one with the proud, violent temper. She was aware that she belonged to the lower class and she resented it, refusing to be judged according to her social status alone. She would often say of the rich, "They're no better than us." She was an attractive blonde with grey eyes, pleasantly plump and bursting with health. She read anything she could lay hands on. She enjoyed singing the latest popular songs, making-up, and going out with friends to the cinema or to the theatre, to see *Roger la Honte* and *Le Maître de Forges*. Always ready for a "bit of fun."

But in those days, in a small town where people's main concern was to learn as much as they could about their neighbors, one was inevitably torn between wanting to "enjoy one's youth" and fearing for one's reputation. My mother tried to live up to the best possible image people could have of her kind: "Factory girls, *but nonetheless* respectable." She went to mass and to Holy Communion, embroidered her trousseau at the local orphanage run by nuns, and never went to the woods alone with a boy. How could she know that her short skirts (she took them up herself), her urchin cut, the "bold" expression in her eyes, and especially the fact that she worked with men, meant that she would never be seen as a "decent young girl," which was what she had always longed to be.

My mother's youth involved trying to escape the dull certainties of her fate: inevitable poverty, the threat of alcoholism, and everything else that happened to a factory girl who had slipped into bad habits (smoking in public, hanging around the streets at night, going out in soiled clothes). The sort of girl that no "respectable young man" would look at twice.

None of her brothers or sisters were spared. Four of them have died over the past twenty-five years. For a long time their frenzied appetite was quenched by alcohol, the men together in cafés, the women alone at home. (Only the youngest sister, who didn't drink, is still alive.) Unless they had had a certain amount to drink, they remained sullen and taciturn. They slogged through their work in silence, "a good employee" or "a charwoman who never gave any cause for complaint." Over the years they got used to being judged solely in terms of how much they had drunk, they were "tipsy" or they were "sloshed." One year, on Whit Saturday, I met my aunt M— on the way back from school. It was her day off and as usual she was going into town with a shopping bag full of empty bottles. She kissed me on both cheeks, swaying slightly, incapable of uttering a single word. My writing would never have been what it is had I not met my aunt that day.

For a woman, marriage was a matter of life or death. It was either the hope of "making it work together" or else hitting rock bottom. So one had to be able to recognize the man who would make a woman happy. Naturally, not a farmer's boy, even one with money, with whom one would end up milking the cows in a village without electricity. My father worked at the rope factory. He was a tall, well-groomed man who definitely had a "style of his own." He didn't drink but saved all his pay for the housekeeping. He had a quiet, cheerful nature and was seven years older than her ("One didn't go for the young lads!"). Smiling and blushing, my mother would tell me: "I was courted quite a bit in my time. Several men proposed to me but it was your father I chose." She used to add: "He didn't look common."

The story of my father's life was no different from my mother's. He came from a large family, his father was a carter, his mother a weaver, and he left school at the age of twelve to start working in the fields. His elder brother had got himself a good job as a railwayman and two of his sisters had married shop assistants. Before that they worked as housemaids: they spoke without raising their voices, moved in a ladylike manner, and never drew attention to themselves in public. True, they enjoyed an air of "respectability" but tended to look down on factory girls like my mother. Her appearance and her ways were too reminiscent of their own world, the one they were leaving behind. In their opinion, my father "could have done better for himself."

They were married in 1928.

In the wedding photograph she looks like a madonna, with pale, regular features, a kiss-curl and a half-veil hugging her head. Heavy breasts and hips; pretty legs (the dress leaves her knees uncovered). She isn't smiling but her face wears a serene expression, a glint of curiosity and amusement in the eyes. He, with his moustache and bow tie, looks much older. His brows are knitted and he looks worried. Maybe he is afraid the photograph will come out wrong. He's got his arm around her waist and she's resting one hand on his shoulder. They are in a country lane, beside a court-yard overgrown with grass. The leaves of two apple trees interlace to form a dome above their heads. A small house is visible in the background. I can conjure up the scene vividly: the dry earth beneath their feet, the loose gravel and the country smell of early summer. But she is not my mother. Stare as I may at the photo-graph, until the faces actually seem to move, all I see is an impenetrable young woman, ill at ease in a costume that could have come straight out of a twenties film. Only the broad hand clutching her gloves and the proud upward tilt of her head tell me it is she.

The young bride was both proud and happy, of that I have very little doubt. But of her desires I know nothing. The first few nights of her married life—she once confided to a sister—she went to bed still wearing her pants under her nightdress. It didn't mean much. In those days, sex was inevitably tinged with shame. Even so, one had to make love, and properly too, if one was "normal."

At first she enjoyed playing the married woman who had settled down, showing off the new china and the embroidered linen, and walking arm-in-arm with her "husband." There were the laughs, the arguments (she didn't know how to cook), the making up (she never sulked for long), and the feeling she was starting a new life. But wages were still low. They had the rent to pay, and the installments on the furniture. They had to economize on everything and ask their parents for vegetables (they had no garden), so in effect they were leading much the same existence as before. They themselves lived their lives differently. Although they both wanted to succeed, he feared the struggle ahead and felt tempted to give in and accept their lot. She, on the other hand, was convinced that they had nothing to lose and that they should try to come up in the world "at any cost." She was proud to be a factory girl but too proud to stay one all her life, dreaming of the only ambition which lay within her reach: running a grocery business. She was the driving force behind their relationship and so he followed her.

In 1931, they took out a loan on a grocery shop and a small adjoining café situated in Lillebonne, an industrial estate of seven thousand inhabitants twenty-five kilometers away from Yvetot. The store lay in the Valley, where nineteenth-century cotton mills ruled people's lives from infancy to death. Even now, to mention the Valley in prewar times is to evoke images of horror: the highest concentration of alcoholics and unmarried mothers, the damp running down the walls, and the babies dying from diarrhea within two hours. My mother was twenty-five at the time. It was here that she must have become the woman that she was, and acquired the expression, the personality, and the manners that I thought had always been hers.

As the business didn't bring enough money, my father used to get jobs working on building sites. Later he was taken on by a refinery in the Basse-Seine, where he ended up as foreman. She ran the shop on her own.

From the very start, she threw herself into it ("a friendly word for every customer," "always in a good humor"), showing remarkable patience ("I could have sold anything!"). She was familiar with the industrial poverty one found in the Valley, having known it herself, if on a lesser scale. She was also aware of her situation and realized that her own livelihood depended on families who were living from hand to mouth.

Not a moment to herself, I'm sure, what with rushing in and out of the shop, the café, and the kitchen, where a little girl had started to grow up. (She was born soon after they moved to the Valley.) Staying open from six in the morning—when the factory girls picked up the milk—to eleven o'clock at night—the last rounds were for the card and billiard players. Being "interrupted" at any moment by customers who would pop in several times a day. She resented earning little more than a factory girl and was worried they would never "make ends meet." On the other hand, she enjoyed a sense of power—after all, didn't she help other families survive by giving them credit?— and she loved to share in the conversations—Oh! the lives that went on in that shop. In short, she felt happy in her new, broadened surroundings.

She gradually became more "civilized." Because she had to go everywhere (the tax office, the town hall) and deal with suppliers and representatives, she learned to watch her language and never went out hatless. Before buying a dress, she would consider whether it was "chic." She hoped, and later knew, that she would never be taken for a "country lass." Besides Delly's popular romances and the Catholic works by Pierre l'Ermite, she took to reading Mauriac, Bernanos, and Colette's "scandalous stories." My father found it more difficult to adapt. His experience as a factory hand had left him with a shy, gauche manner and somehow he never quite felt at home behind the bar.

There were the black years of the economic crisis, the strikes, Léon Blum ("the first man to be on the side of the workers"), the social reforms, and the late-night parties in the café. There were the visits from her relatives—they laid down mattresses in all the rooms—who returned home loaded with provisions (she was a generous person and, after all, the only one to have made it). There were also the arguments with "the other side of the family." And then the sorrow. Their little girl had a gay, excitable nature. In one photograph she looks tall for her age, with skinny legs and knobby knees. She is laughing, one hand raised to her forehead to keep the sun out of her eyes. Another photograph shows her at her cousin's confirmation. Although her face wears a serious expression, she is playing with her fingers, spread out in front of her. She died in 1938, three days before Easter. They only wanted one baby as they felt the child would be happier alone.

There was the sorrow, over which a veil was slowly drawn, the stark silence of depression, the prayers, and the belief that their little girl "had gone to heaven." And then, in early 1940, life once more: she was expecting a second child. I was to be born in September.

I believe I am writing about my mother because it is my turn to bring her into the world.

It was two months ago that I started this book and wrote "My mother died on Monday 7 April" on a blank sheet of paper. I can accept that sentence now. When I read it, the emotions I feel are the same as if someone else had written it. But I can't bear going near the hospital and the old people's home, or suddenly remembering details about the last day of her life. Initially, I thought I would find it easy to write. In actual fact, I spend a lot of time reflecting on what I have to say and on the choice and sequence of words, as if there existed only one immutable order which would convey the truth about my mother (although what this truth involves I am unable to say). When I am writing, the only thing that matters to me is to find that particular order.

Then the exodus: she walked all the way to Niort with some neighbors, sleeping in barns and drinking the local wine, then cycled back on her own, passing the German roadblocks, to have her baby at home one month later. She wasn't afraid and was so dirty when she got back that my father didn't recognize her.

Under the Occupation, life in the Valley centered on their shop and the hope of getting fresh supplies. She tried to feed everyone, especially large families, because her natural pride encouraged her to be kind and helpful to others. During the bombing, saying she preferred to die "in her own home," she wouldn't take refuge in the public shelters carved out of the hillside. In the afternoon, between warnings, she would take me for a walk in my stroller, claiming the fresh air would do me good. Those were the days of easy friendship: sitting on a bench in the public park while my father was left in charge of the empty shop, she would get talking to demure young women who sat knitting in front of the sand pit. The English and the Americans entered Lillebonne. The tanks crossed the Valley, distributing chocolate and packets of orange powder, which one picked up from the dust. Every evening, the café packed with soldiers, maybe the occasional brawl, but all the same a time of rejoicing and, of course knowing how to say "shit for you." Afterwards she spoke of the war like a novel, the great story of her life. (Oh! how she loved *Gone with the Wind*.) I think she saw the war years as a break in the struggle to succeed. With so much misery around, fighting for social advancement had lost all meaning.

The woman of that time cut a handsome figure, with a fine head of hair, which she dyed red. She had a formidable voice and would often shout in thunderous tones. She liked to laugh too—a deep, throaty laugh, which revealed her teeth and gums. She sang as she did the ironing—*Le Temps des Cerises, Riquita Jolie Fleur de Java*. She wore turbans and had two favorite dresses, a summer one with big, blue stripes and a soft, beige one made of seersucker. She powdered her face with a puff in a mirror above the sink and dabbed perfume behind her ear. When she put on lipstick, she always started with the heart-shaped bit in the middle. She turned to face the wall when she fastened her corset. Her flesh bulged through the crisscross of laces, joined together at her waist by a knot and a small rosette. I knew every detail of her body. I thought that I would grow up to become her.

One Sunday they are having a picnic on the edge of an embankment, near the woods. I remember being between them, in a warm nest of voices, flesh, and continual laughter. On the way back we were caught in an air raid. I am sitting on the crossbar of my father's bike, while she rides down the slope ahead of us, her back straight, the seat firmly wedged between her buttocks. I am afraid of the shells, afraid too that she will die. I believe we were both in love with my mother.

In 1945, they left the Valley, where the foggy climate made me cough and stunted my growth, and moved back to Yvetot. Life in the postwar period was more difficult than during the war. Food was still rationed and those who had "cashed in on the black market" were slowly emerging. While she was waiting to take over a new business, she would walk me round the streets of the town center, littered with debris, or would take me to pray in the chapel, set up in a concert hall to replace the church which had burned down. My father got a job filling in the holes left by the shells. They lived in two rooms without electricity, with the furniture dismantled and stacked up against the wall.

Three months later she was a new woman, running a business in a semirural district that the war had passed by. As before, they had taken over a general store and a small café. All they had was a tiny kitchen, an upstairs bedroom, and two attic rooms, where one could eat and sleep in relative privacy. On the other hand, there was a large courtyard, a cider press, and several barns for storing firewood, straw and hay. The main advantage, however, was that most customers could afford to pay cash. Although my father ran the café, he managed to find time to look after the garden, keep a few rabbits and hens, and make apple cider, which we sold to the customers. After twenty years of being a worker, he returned to a semirural lifestyle. She was in charge of the store, the accounts, and the orders and reigned supreme over all money matters. Over the years they came to enjoy a higher standard of living than the other working-class people around them. They eventually succeeded in buying the premises, as well as the small adjoining house.

During the first few years, former customers from Lillebonne came over to see them in the summer holidays. They arrived by coach, bringing their whole families with them. There was a lot of hugging and crying. At mealtimes, they set up the café tables in long rows, sang songs, and reminisced about the Occupation. They stopped coming in the early fifties. She said: "That's all in the past, one must look to the future now."

Images of her, aged between forty and forty-six:
- one winter morning, she has the nerve to enter the classroom and ask the schoolmistress to find the woolen scarf which I had lost in the lavatories and which had cost her a pretty penny (I remembered the price for a long time);
- at the seaside one summer, she is fishing for mussels with a sister-in-law younger than herself. Her dress—black stripes on a mauve background—has been rolled up and knotted at the front. Several times during the day, they walk over to a café set up in a hut on the beach and order aperitifs and pastries, laugh-

ing all the time;

- in church, she sang hymns to the Virgin in a loud, booming voice—"One day I shall meet her in heaven, up in heaven." It made me want to cry and I hated her for it;
- she wore brightly colored dresses and a black woolen suit. She read *Confidences* and *La Mode du Jour*, both popular women's weeklies. She put her soiled sanitary towels in a corner of the attic until washing day—Tuesday;
- when I stared at her, she got cross: "Why are you looking at me? Do you want to buy me or something?";
- on Sunday afternoons, she would lie down in her slip and stockings. She let me crawl into bed next to her. She fell asleep quickly while I read, huddled up against her back;
- once, at a confirmation reception, she got drunk and was sick right in front of me. After that, every time there was a party, I eyed the arm resting on the table, and the hand holding the glass, and prayed with all my might that she wouldn't raise it to her lips.

She had put on a lot of weight; she was fifteen stone. She ate voraciously and stored sugar lumps in her apron pocket. Unknown to my father, she purchased some slimming pills from a chemist's in Rouen to lose weight. She cut out bread, as well as butter, but lost only twenty pounds.

She slammed doors. She banged the chairs when she stacked them on to the tables before sweeping the floor. Everything she did was done noisily. She didn't put things down, she seemed to throw them.

One could tell whether she was upset simply by looking at her face. In private she didn't mince her words and told us straight out what she thought. She called me a beast, a slut, and a bitch, or told me I was "unpleasant." She would often hit me, usually by slapping my face, or occasionally punching my shoulders ("I could have killed her!"). Five minutes later, she would take me into her arms and I was her "poppet."

She bought me toys and books under any pretext, a party, a trip into town, or a slight temperature. She took me to the dentist's, the lung specialist, and made sure I had good shoes, warm clothes, and all the right stationery I needed for class (she had enrolled me at a private establishment run by nuns, and not at the local primary school). If I mentioned that one of the other girls had an unbreakable slate, she would immediately ask me if I wanted one: "I wouldn't want them to think you're not as good as the others." Her overriding concern was to give me everything she hadn't had. But this involved so much work, so much worrying about money, and an approach to children's happiness so radically different from her own education, that she couldn't help saying: "You know, we spend a lot of money on you" or "Look at everything you've got, and you're still not happy!"

When I think of my mother's violent temper, outbursts of affection, and reproachful attitude, I try not to see them as facets of her personality but to relate them to her own story and social background. This way of writing, which seems to bring me closer to the truth, relieves me of the dark, heavy burden of personal remembrance by establishing a more objective approach. And yet something deep down inside refuses to yield and wants me to remember my mother purely in emotional terms—affection or tears—without searching for an explanation.

She was a working mother, which meant that her first duty lay with the customers who were our livelihood. I wasn't allowed to interrupt her when she was serving in the shop. (I can remember standing behind the kitchen door, waiting for a few strands of embroidery silk, permission to go and play, and so on.) If I made too much noise, she would burst into the room, slap my face and go back to the counter without uttering a single word. I learnt at an early age how to behave with the customers: "Say hallo in a nice, clear voice," "Don't eat or quarrel in front of them," "Don't criticize anybody." I was also taught to view them with distrust: "Never believe what they say," "Keep an eye on them when they're alone in the shop." She had two expressions, one for the customers and one for us. When the bell rang, she went in and played her part, her face beaming, a paragon of patience, asking people the ritual questions about their health, the children, and the garden. Back in the kitchen, she flopped into a chair and the smile faded. She remained speechless for a few moments, exhausted by the role she had taken on. She felt both excited and depressed by the idea that she worked so hard for people who, she was sure, would stop coming to her as soon as they "found somewhere cheaper."

She was a mother everyone knew, a sort of public figure. At school, when I was sent to the blackboard, they would say: "Suppose your mother sells ten packets of coffee each at . . ." (Naturally, they never mentioned the other possibility, which was equally likely: "Suppose your mother sells three aperitifs each at . . .")

She was always in a rush. She never had time to do the cooking and look after the house "properly," sewing on a button seconds before I left for school, or ironing her blouse on a corner of the kitchen table before slipping it on. After five o'clock in the morning, she scrubbed the floor and unpacked the cardboard boxes. In summer she weeded the rose beds before opening the shop. She was a quick, energetic worker and the chores that gave her the most satisfaction were, strangely enough, the most strenuous ones, the ones she cursed, like washing the sheets and scouring the bedroom floor with steel wool. She found it impossible to lie down or read a book without giving an excuse, for instance, "I think I deserve a little rest now." (And even then, if she was interrupted by a customer, she would hide her novel under a pile of clothes that needed darning.) The arguments she had with my father always centered on the same subject: the amount of work they carried out respectively. She used to complain: "I'm the one who does everything around here."

My father would read only the local newspaper. He didn't go to places where he didn't feel "at home" and said of many things that they were not for him. He liked gardening, playing cards and dominoes, and doing odd jobs around the house. He didn't care about speaking properly and continued to use expressions in the local dialect. She, on the other hand, tried to avoid making grammatical mistakes and chose her words carefully. For instance, she no longer said "serviette" but "napkin." Occasionally, in the course of the conversation, she would throw in an unfamiliar expression she had read somewhere or picked up from "educated people." She would speak hesitantly, her face flushed with embarrassment, afraid of making a mistake, while my father laughed and poked fun at her "highfalutin words." Once she felt confident, she took pleasure in repeating them several times. If she felt they were metaphors—"He wore his heart on his sleeve" or "We're only birds of passage"—she would smile as she said them, hoping maybe they would sound less pretentious. She loved "style," anything "dressy," and the Printemps department store, more chic, she thought, than the Nouvelles Galeries. Naturally, she was just as impressed as he was by the carpets and paintings that adorned the eye specialist's surgery, but she always tried to conceal her embarrassment. One of her favorite expressions was "I had the cheek" to do this or that. When my father remarked on a new dress or her careful makeup before she left the house, she would reply sharply: "After all, one must keep up one's position!"

She longed to learn the rules of good behavior and was

always worrying about social conventions, fearful of doing the wrong thing. She longed to know what was in fashion, what was new, the names of famous writers, the recent films on release—although she didn't go to the cinema, she hadn't time—and the names of the flowers in gardens. She listened attentively when people spoke of something she didn't know, out of curiosity, and also because she wanted to show that she was eager to learn. In her opinion, self-improvement was first and foremost a question of learning and nothing was more precious than knowledge. (She would often say: "One must occupy one's mind.") Books were the only things she handled with care. She washed her hands before touching them.

Through me, she continued to satisfy her thirst for knowledge. In the evening, over dinner, she would make me talk about school, the teachers, and the subjects I was taught. She liked using the same expressions as me, such as "break," "PE," and "prep." She expected me to correct her when she had used the wrong word. She no longer asked me if I wanted my "tea" but if I wanted my "dinner." She took me to

Rouen, to see the museum and the other historical monuments, and to Villequier, to visit the graves of Victor Hugo's family. She was full of admiration for everything. She read the same books I read, the ones recommended by the local bookshop. Sometimes she browsed through Le Hérisson,[†] left behind by one of the customers, exclaiming in light-hearted tones: "It's silly but one reads it just the same!" (When she took me to the museum, it wasn't so much for the pleasure of admiring Egyptian vases, but for the satisfaction of helping me acquire the knowledge and the tastes that she attributed to cultivated people. Sacrificing *Confidences* and spending the day with Dickens, Daudet, and the recumbent statues in the cathedral was no doubt more for my benefit than for hers.)

I thought her a cut above my father because she seemed closer to the schoolmistresses and teachers than he did. Everything about my mother—her author-

---

[†] A highly popular satirical weekly founded in 1937 and named after the house mascot, a hedgehog, which proudly adorns the front page. Printed on green paper—"the color of optimism," to quote the editor—*Le Hérisson* offers a blend of satire, political comment, humorous articles, cartoons, and quizzes.

ity, her hopes, and her ambitions—was geared to the very concept of education. We shared an intimacy centered on books, the poetry I read to her, and the pastries in the teashop at Rouen, from which he was excluded. He took me to the funfair, to the circus, and to see Fernandel's films. He taught me how to ride a bicycle and recognize the garden vegetables. With him I had fun, with her I had "conversations." Of the two, she was the dominating figure, the one who represented authority.

The images I have of her as she approached her fifties are those of a tense, irritable woman. Still the same personality—lively, energetic, and generous, still the blonde or reddish hair, but often a strained expression on her face when she didn't have to smile at customers. The slightest incident or remark would be an excuse for her to pick a quarrel with her brothers and sisters, or release her anger against their living conditions (small local businesses were threatened by the shops in the new town center). After my grandmother died, she continued to wear mourning for a long time and took to attending early-morning mass. Something "Roman-esque" in her died.

1952. Her forty-sixth summer. We have come over by coach to spend the day in Étretat. She is climbing up the cliff, moving through the long grass in her blue crêpe dress, the one with the big flowers, which she slipped into behind the rocks. She left home in her mourning suit because of the neighbors. She reaches the top after me, breathless, the beads of sweat glistening through her makeup. She hasn't had her period for two months.

During my adolescence I broke away from her and there remained only the struggle between us. In the world where she grew up, the very idea that young girls could enjoy sexual freedom was unthinkable. Those who did were doomed for life. Sex was either presented as a saucy business unfit for "virgin ears" or else it served to dictate moral standards—people behaved "properly" or "improperly." She told me nothing about the facts of life and I would never have dreamed of ask-ing her. In those days, curiosity carried the seeds of vice. I can remember the feeling of panic when I had to confess that I had my period and say the word in front of her for the first time. I can also remember her acute embarrassment as she handed me a sanitary towel, without explaining what to do with it.

She didn't like to see me grow up. When she saw me undressed, my body seemed to repel her. No doubt she saw my breasts and hips as a threat and was afraid I would start running after boys and lose interest in my studies. She wanted me to stay a child, saying I was thirteen a week before my fourteenth birthday and making me wear pleated skirts, ankle socks, and low-heeled shoes. Until I was eighteen practically all our arguments revolved around my choice of clothes and her forbidding me to go out. For instance, she insisted on my wearing a girdle when I left the house: "That way, you'll be dressed properly." She would fly into a terrible rage—"You're not going out like that!"—for apparently no reason (a dress, a new hairstyle) and although these outbursts were excessive, they seemed perfectly normal to me. We both knew what to expect from each other: she knew I longed to seduce the boys, I knew she was terrified I would "have an accident," in other words, that I would start to sleep around and get pregnant.

Sometimes I imagined her death would have meant nothing to me.

As I write, I see her sometimes as a "good," sometimes as a "bad" mother. To get away from these contrasting views, which come from my earliest childhood, I try to describe and explain her life as if I were writing about someone else's mother and a daughter who wasn't me. Although I try to be as objective as possible, certain expressions, such as "If you ever have an accident . . ." will always strike a sensitive chord in me, while others remain totally abstract, for instance, "the denial of one's own body and sexuality." When I remember these expressions, I experience the same feeling of disillusion I had when I was sixteen. Fleetingly, I confuse the woman who influenced me most with an African mother pinning her daughter's arms behind her back while the village midwife slices off the girl's clitoris.

I stopped trying to copy her. I felt drawn to the feminine ideal portrayed in L'*Echo de la Mode*. The women one read about were slim and discreet; they were good cooks and called their little girls "darling." They reminded me of the middle-class mothers whose daughters were my companions at school. I found my own mother's attitude brash. I averted my eyes when she uncorked a bottle, holding it locked between her knees. I was ashamed of her brusque manners and speech, especially when I realized how alike we were. I blamed her for being someone who I, by moving into new circles, no longer wanted to be. I discovered there was a world of difference between wanting to be educated and actually acquiring that knowledge. My mother needed an encyclopedia to say who Van Gogh was. She knew the classics only by name. My school curriculum was a mystery to her. Because of my strong admiration for her, I couldn't help feeling that she—much more than my father—had let me down, by not being able to lend me her support and by leaving me defenseless in a strange, new world, where the other girls' drawing-rooms were lined with books. All she had to offer me were her anxiety and her suspicion: "Who were you with?" "Are you getting your work done?"

We spoke to each other in quarrelsome tones. Her efforts to revive our former intimacy—"you know you can tell your mother everything"—were met by silence because I realized this was no longer possible. If I showed enthusiasm for subjects other than school (sports, travel, parties) or if I discussed politics (it was during the Algerian war), at first she would listen attentively, flattered to be my confidante, then would snap angrily: "Stop worrying about all that, you know school comes first."

I began to scorn social conventions, religious practices, and money. I copied out poems by Rimbaud and Prévert, stuck photographs of James Dean on the front of my exercise books, and played *La Mauvaise Réputation* by Georges Brassens. I identified with anonymous artists. In short, I was bored. My teenage crisis smacked of romanticism, as if my parents had come from a bourgeois background. For my mother, rebellion meant only one thing—the denial of poverty—and called for only one possible course of action: get a job, earn money, and work one's way up the social ladder. As a result, she criticized me bitterly, an attitude which was as incomprehensible to me as my behavior was to her: "If we'd packed you off to a factory at the age of twelve, it'd be a different story. You don't know how lucky you are." She would often say of me in bitter tones: "Look at her! She goes to a convent school and yet she's no better than the rest of them."

Sometimes she saw her own daughter as a class rival.

I longed to leave home. She agreed to let me go to the *lycée* in Rouen and later to London. She was ready to make any sacrifice if it meant a better life for me. Better than she had known. She even consented to make the greatest sacrifice of all, which was to part with me. Away from her scrutiny, I rushed headlong into everything she had forbidden. I stuffed myself with food, then I stopped eating for weeks, until I reached a state of euphoria. Then I understood what it was to be free. I forgot about our arguments. When I was studying at the arts faculty, I saw her in a simpler light, without the shouting and the violence. I was both certain of her love for me and aware of one blatant injustice: she spent all day selling milk and potatoes so that I could sit in a lecture hall and learn about Plato.

Although I didn't miss her, I was always pleased to see her again. I usually came back home after an unhappy love affair, which I couldn't talk about to her, even if she whispered secrets to me about the local girls (who was going out with whom, who had just had a miscarriage, and so on). It was somehow agreed that, although I was old enough to hear about these things, they would never concern me personally.

When I arrived home, she would be serving behind the counter. The customers would all turn round. She would blush faintly and smile. We would embrace in the kitchen, after the last customer had left. She would inquire about the journey and my studies, adding, "You must give me your washing" and "I've kept all the papers since you left." We behaved towards each other with kindness, almost shyness, as is the case with people who have stopped living together. For many years, my relationship with her consisted of a series of homecomings.

53

My father underwent gastrointestinal surgery. He tired easily and hadn't enough strength to lift the crates. She took over and did both their jobs without complaining. She seemed to enjoy the responsibility. After I left home, they argued less and she grew closer to him, affectionately calling him "Pop" and showing more indulgence for his little ways, like smoking: "After all, he's entitled to a bit of pleasure." On Sunday afternoons, in summer, they went for a drive in the country or dropped in to see relatives. In winter, after vespers, she visited the elderly. She came back through the town center, stopping to watch television in a shopping arcade where the local teenagers gathered when they came out of the cinema.

The customers said she was still a handsome woman. She continued to wear high heels and dye her hair, but now she had bifocals and a touch of down around the chin, which she burnt off in private. (My father noted these changes with secret amusement, pleased to see her catch up on the years that separated them.) She gave up her flimsy, brightly colored dresses and took to wearing grey and black suits, even during the warm weather. She stopped tucking her blouse into her skirt, so as to be more comfortable.

Until I was twenty, I thought I was responsible for her growing old.

Nobody knows that I am writing about her. But then, in a sense, I feel I am not writing about her. It's more like experiencing again the times and places we shared when she was alive. When I am at home, I occasionally come across things that used to belong to her, like her thimble, the day before yesterday, the one she always wore on her crooked finger, the result of an accident at the rope factory. Suddenly the reality of her death overwhelms me and I am back in the real world, the one where she will no longer be. In these circumstances, to publish a book can mean nothing except the definitive death of my mother. How I long to curse the people who ask me with a smile: "And when is your next book coming out?"

Until I married, I still belonged to her, even when we were living apart. When relatives or customers asked after me, she would reply: "The girl's got plenty of time to get married. At her age, there's no great rush." Seconds later, she would take it all back, protesting: "I don't want to keep her. It's a woman's life to have a husband and children." She blushed and started to shake when I announced one summer that I planned to marry a political-science student from Bordeaux. She tried to find excuses, showing the same provincial distrust that she condemned in others: "The boy's not from our part of the world." Later, she relaxed and felt happier about my situation. After all, she lived in a small town where marriage said a lot about one's social status and nobody could say I had "ended up with a worker." We entered a new period of intimacy, revolving around the pots and pans to buy and the preparations for the "big day" and, later, around the children. From then on, these were the only things that brought us together.

My husband and I had the same level of education. We discussed Jean-Paul Sartre and freedom, we went to see Antonioni's *L'Avventura*, we shared the same left-wing views, and yet we weren't from the same background. In his family, they weren't exactly rich but they had been to university, they were good conversationalists, and they played bridge. My mother-in-law was the same age as my own mother: she still had a good figure, a smooth complexion, and carefully manicured hands. She could sight-read piano music and knew how to "entertain." (She was the type of woman one saw in drawing-room comedy on television: in her fifties, disarmingly naïve, a string of pearls on a silk blouse.)

My mother had mixed feelings about my husband's family. Although she admired their style, their manners, and their education, and was naturally proud to see her daughter fit in, she feared that beneath their icy politeness they held her in contempt. The feeling that she wasn't worthy of them, a feeling which in her eyes applied also to me (perhaps it needed another generation for this to pass), was blatantly obvious in the advice she gave me on the eve of my wedding day: "Make sure you're a good housewife, otherwise he might send you back." Of my mother-in-law, she once said a few years ago: "Anyone can see she wasn't brought up the way we were."

Because she feared people wouldn't love her for what she was, she hoped they would love her for what she could give. She insisted on helping us through our last year at college and was always asking what we wanted as a present. The other family had originality and a sense of humor. They felt they owed us nothing.

We moved to Bordeaux, and then to Annecy, where my husband was offered a senior executive position. What with cooking the meals, bringing up a young child, and teaching at a *lycée* in the mountains forty kilometers from home, I too became a woman with no time to spare. I hardly thought about my mother, she seemed as far away as the life I'd had before I married. I replied briefly to the letters she sent us every fortnight. She started with "My dearest children," and always apologized for not being able to help us, living so far apart. I saw her once a year, for a few days in summer. I described Annecy, our flat, and the ski resorts. In my father's presence, she remarked: "The two of you are doing fine, that's all that matters." When I was alone with her, she obviously wanted me to confide in her and talk about my husband and our relationship. She seemed disappointed by my silence because it offered no answer to the question that was probably foremost in her mind: "Does he at least make her happy?"

In 1967 my father had a coronary and died four days later. I cannot describe these events because I have already done so in a different book and there can be no other narrative, no other possible choice and order of words to explain what happened. All I can say is that I remember my mother washing my father's face after his death, easing his arms into the sleeves of a freshly laundered shirt and slipping him into his Sunday best. As she dressed him, she lulled him with soft, gentle words, as if he were a child one bathes and sends to sleep. When I saw her neat, simple movements, I realized she had always known he would die first. The first night following his death, she lay down beside him in bed. Until the undertakers removed his body, she popped upstairs to see him between customers, just as she had done during his four-day illness.

After the funeral, she looked sad and weary and confessed to me: "It's tough to lose one's man." She continued to run the business as before. (I have just read in a newspaper that "despair is a luxury." The book I started writing after my mother's death—a book that I have both the time and the ability to write—may also be seen as a form of luxury.)

She saw more of the family, spent hours chatting to young women in the shop, and kept the café open till late because the local youth had taken to meeting there. She developed a keen appetite and put on weight again. She had become quite talkative and was inclined to share her secrets like a young girl. She was flattered to tell me that two widowers had shown an interest in her. During the events of May 1968, she exclaimed over the phone: "Things are happening over here too, you know!" Later that summer, she sided with the Establishment. (She was furious when the leftists vandalized the top Parisian delicatessen Fauchon, which she saw very much like her own shop, only bigger.)

In her letters, she said she was far too busy to be bored, but in actual fact she hoped for only one thing, to come and live with me. One day she ventured: "If I moved into your place, I could look after the house."

In Annecy, I thought of her with a guilty conscience. Although we lived in a large, comfortable house and had a family of two, none of it was for her benefit. I imagined her leading a pampered existence with her two grandsons. I felt sure she would enjoy this sort of life because she had wanted it for me. In 1970, she sold the business as private property—no one would buy it as an ongoing concern—and she came to live with us.

It was a mild day in January. She arrived with the moving van in the afternoon while I was still out teaching. When I got back home, I caught sight of her in the garden, her arms clasped around her one-year-old grandson. She was keeping an eye on the men moving the furniture and the last remaining boxes of groceries from the shop. Her hair had turned quite white. She was laughing, bursting with energy as usual. She shouted to me from a distance: "You're just in time!" Suddenly my heart sank when I realized: "From now on, I shall have to live my whole life in front of her."

At first, she wasn't as happy as we had expected. All of a sudden, her shopkeeper's life was over. No more financial worries and long working hours, but on the other hand, no more familiar faces and chatting to customers. Worst of all, maybe, she no longer had the satisfaction of earning "her own" money. In Annecy she was just a "granny." Nobody knew her in town and she only had us to talk to. Her world had suddenly shrunk and lost its sparkle. Now she felt she was a nobody.

Living with her children meant sharing a lifestyle of which she was proud (she would say to relatives: "They've done so well for themselves!"). It also meant remembering not to dry the dishcloths on the radiator in the hall, "taking care of things" (records, crystal vases), and "observing personal hygiene" (blowing the boys' noses on a clean handkerchief). We discovered that the things we considered unimportant meant a lot to her: everyday news items, crime, accidents, being on good terms with one's neighbors, and trying not to "trouble" people. (We even laughed at her attitude, which upset her.) Living with us was like living in a world that welcomed her and rejected her at the same time. One day she said angrily: "I don't think I belong here."

And so she wouldn't answer the phone when it rang next to her. If her son-in-law was watching football on television, she would make a point of knocking on the door before entering the living room. She was always asking for work—"Well, if there's nothing to do, I might as well leave then"—adding with a touch of irony, "After all, I've got to earn my keep!" The two of us would argue about her attitude and I blamed her for deliberately humiliating herself. It took me a long time to realize that the feeling of unease my mother experienced in my own house was no different from what I had felt as a teenager when I was introduced to people "a cut above us." (As if only the "lower classes" suffered from inequalities which others choose to ignore.) I also realized that the cultural supremacy my husband and I enjoyed—reading Le Monde, listening to Bach—was distorted by my mother into a form of economic supremacy, based on the exploitation of labor: putting herself in the position of an employee was her way of rebelling.

After a while, she grew accustomed to her lifestyle, channeling her energy and her enthusiasm towards looking after her grandsons and helping to clean the house. She wanted to relieve me of all the household chores. She regretted having to let me do the shopping and the cooking, and start up the washing machine, which she was afraid to use. She resented having to share the only part of the house where her talents were acknowledged and where she knew she could be of use. As in the old days, she was the mother who refuses to be helped, using the same reproachful tones when she saw me working with my hands: "Leave that alone, you've got better things to do." (When I was ten years old, this meant doing my homework; now it meant preparing my lessons and behaving like an intellectual.)

We had gone back to addressing each other in that particular tone of speech—a cross between exasperation and perpetual resentment—which led people to believe, wrongly, that we were always arguing. I would recognize that tone of conversation between a mother and her daughter anywhere in the world.

She adored both her grandsons, to whom she was devoted. In the afternoon, she strapped the younger one into his stroller and set off to explore the town. She visited the churches, went for a stroll round the old part of town, and spent hours in the amusement park, returning only at nightfall. In summer she took the boys to the heights of Annecy-le-Vieux, showed them the lake, and satisfied their craving for sweets, ice cream, and rides on the merry-go-round. She got talking to people in parks and would meet up with them regularly. She became friendly with the lady who ran the local baker's shop. She invented a whole new world for herself.

Now she read *Le Monde* and *Le Nouvel Observateur*, showed an interest in antiques—"It must be worth a lot"—and dropped in on friends "to take tea" ("I don't like the stuff, but I haven't told them that," she would remark, laughing). She was careful not to use bad language and tried to handle things "gently," keeping a close watch on herself and a tight rein on her temper. One could even say that she was proud of acquiring late in life the knowledge that most middle-class women of her generation had been taught in their youth, that is, how to "manage a household."

Now she never wore black, only light colors.

In a photograph taken in September 1971, her face is beaming, crowned by a head of snow-white hair. She has lost weight and is wearing a Rodier blouse printed with arabesque motifs. Her hands are resting on the shoulders of her two grandsons, who are standing in front of her. They are the same broad, folded hands to be seen in her wedding photograph.

In the mid-1970s, she followed us to a new town that was still under development, located on the outskirts of Paris, where my husband had been offered a better job. We lived in a house that was part of a new residential estate built in the center of a plain. The shops and schools were two kilometers away. The only time we saw the neighbors was in the evening. On weekends, they washed the car and put up shelves in the garage. It was an empty, soulless place where one drifted aimlessly, devoid of thought and emotion.

She never got used to living there. In the afternoons she would wander along the deserted roads, named after familiar flowers: Daffodil Lane, Cornflower Grove, or Rose Walk. She wrote many letters to her friends in Annecy and to the family. Sometimes she walked as far as the huge shopping center that lay beyond the motorway, treading rutted lanes where the passing cars splashed her legs with mud. She came home with a strained expression on her face. She resented being dependent on me and the car whenever she needed to buy something—a pair of stockings—or go somewhere—the hairdresser's, Sunday mass, and so on. She became irritable and would complain crossly: "I can't spend all day reading!" When we bought a dishwasher, so depriving her of an occupation, she felt humiliated more than anything else: "What am I going to do now?" She spoke to only one person in the housing estate, a West Indian woman who worked in an office.

After six months, she decided to return to Yvetot once more. She moved into a small, ground floor flat for elderly people, not far from the town center. She was happy to be independent again. She enjoyed seeing her youngest sister (the others had died), former customers, and also married nieces who invited her to confirmations and other family gatherings. She borrowed books from the local library and in October made the pilgrimage to Lourdes together with the other parishioners. But gradually, without an occupation, her life fell into a forced routine and the fact that all her neighbors were senior citizens annoyed her intensely (naturally, she refused to have anything to do with the "old people's club"). I am sure too that she felt secretly frustrated: the people of the town where she had spent fifty years of her life, the only people who really mattered to her, would never witness the success of her daughter's family.

The flat in Yvetot was to be the last place of her own. It consisted of a rather dark room, a kitchen area giving on to a small back garden, a niche for the bed and bedside table, a bathroom, and an intercom connected to the caretaker's lodge. The atmosphere there seemed to stifle one's movements. Not that it mattered, there wasn't anything to do except sit down, watch television, and wait until dinnertime. Whenever I went to see her, she would look around her, muttering: "I'd be a fool to complain." I felt she was still too young to be there.

We sat facing each other over lunch. At first we had so much to talk about that we kept interrupting each other: our health, the boys' school reports, the new shops that had opened, the coming holidays, and so on. And then, suddenly, silence. As usual, she would try to pick up the conversation, venturing, "Oh by the way . . ." It occurred to me on one of these visits that her flat was the only place where she had lived without me since I was born. Just as I was leaving, she would produce some administrative document that needed explaining, or start searching for a cleaning or beauty tip she had put aside for me.

Rather than go and see her, I preferred it when she came over to our place: it seemed easier to fit her into our life for a couple of weeks than to share three hours of her empty existence. She rushed over as soon as we invited her. We had left the housing estate and moved to the old village, which was beside the new town. My mother liked this place. She would be standing on the station platform, usually in a red suit, holding a suitcase, which she refused to let me carry. As soon as she had unpacked, she would be out weeding the flower-beds. In summer she spent a month with us in the Nièvre. She would wander off on her own along country lanes and would return laden with blackberries, her legs scratched by the brambles. She never said, "I'm too old to . . ." (go fishing with the boys, take them to the funfair, stay up late, and so on).

Around half past six one evening in December 1979, as she was crossing the N15, she was run over by a Citroën CX which drove through the traffic lights on the pedestrian crossing. (The article published in the local newspaper implied that the driver had been unlucky. It mentioned that "visibility had been impaired owing to recent rainfall" and suggested that "the glare of the cars coming in the opposite direction, together with a number of other factors, may explain why the driver failed to see the seventy-year-old woman.") The accident left her with a broken leg and multiple head injuries. The surgeon at the clinic was confident she would pull through thanks to her strong constitution. She struggled in her coma, trying to wrench the drip away from her body and lift her plastered leg. She shouted to her sister—the blonde one who had been dead twenty years—to watch out, a car was coming straight at her. I looked at her bare shoulders and her body, which for the first time I saw defenseless and in pain. I felt I was standing in front of the young woman who had suffered in giving birth to me one night during the war. With a shock, I realized she could die.

She recovered and regained the use of her broken leg. She was determined to win the case against the driver of the CX and underwent all the medical examinations with brazen resolve. She felt proud when people told her how lucky she had been, as if the car hurtling towards her had been an obstacle which, as usual, she had managed to overcome.

She had changed. She started laying the table much earlier, at eleven o'clock in the morning and half past six in the evening. All she read was *France Dimanche*[†] and the photo-romances passed on to her by a former customer (she hid these in the dresser when I came to see her). She switched on the television when she got up—in those days there were no programs, just the

† One of the more lurid Sunday tabloids.

test-card and background music—left it on all day, barely glancing at it, and fell asleep in front of the set at night. She became irritable, saying about minor inconveniences, "It's disgusting": a ten-centime increase in the price of bread or a pleated skirt she had to iron. She was inclined to panic if she received a circular from her pension fund, or a leaflet announcing she had won a prize—"I didn't send in for anything!" When she talked about Annecy and taking the boys round the old part of town, or feeding the swans on the lake, she was on the verge of tears. Her letters were shorter and less frequent than before, she seemed to have run out of words. A strange smell clung to her flat.

Things started happening to her. The train she was waiting for on the station platform had already left. When she went out to buy something, she discovered all the shops were closed. Her keys kept disappearing. The mail-order firm *La Redoute* sent her articles she hadn't asked for. She turned against her relatives in Yvetot, accusing them of prying into her financial affairs, and refused to see them. One day, she told me over the phone: "I'm sick to death of going round in circles in this bloody flat." She seemed to brace herself against invisible threats.

The month of July 1983 was scorching, even in Normandy. She stopped drinking and lost her appetite, claiming that the drugs she took provided enough nourishment. One day she fainted in the sun and was taken to the medical service of the old people's home. A few days later, after she had been fed and rehydrated, she felt better and asked to go home; "Otherwise," she said, "I'll jump out of the window." According to the doctor, she could no longer be left on her own. He advised me to put her into an old people's home. I rejected this solution.

At the beginning of September, I went over to fetch her in the car. I had decided that she would move in with me. By then I had separated from my husband and was living with my two sons. As I was driving along, I thought, "Now I'll be able to look after her" (just as in my childhood days: "When I grow up, I'll take her around the world, we'll visit the Louvre," and so on). It was a lovely day. She looked perfectly serene, sitting in the front of the car, her handbag in her lap. As usual, we talked about the boys, their studies, and my job.

She was in a cheerful frame of mind and entertained me with stories about the women who had shared her room at the hospital. She made only one odd remark, about one of the other patients: "A real bitch, I could have slapped her face!" That was the last time I can remember seeing my mother happy.

And here her story stops for there was no longer a place for her in society. She was slowly turning insane. She was suffering from Alzheimer's Disease, the name given by the doctors to a form of senile dementia. Over the past few days, I have found it more and more difficult to write, possibly because I would like never to reach this point. And yet I know I shall have no peace of mind until I find the words that will reunite the demented woman she had become with the strong, radiant woman she once was.

She got confused by the different rooms in the house and would ask me angrily how to get to her own bedroom. She started losing things—"I can't put my hands on it"—and was astonished to find them in places where she claimed she had never put them. She demanded that I give her some sewing or ironing or even some vegetables to peel, but as soon as she started on something, she lost patience and gave up. She seemed to live in a state of perpetual restlessness. Although she longed for new occupations—watching television, having lunch, going out in the garden—they never gave her the slightest satisfaction.

In the afternoon, she settled down at the living room table with her writing pad and her address book, like she used to. She started several letters but, after an hour, found she couldn't go on and tore up everything she had written. One of these letters, written in November, read: "Dear Paulette, I am still lost in my world of darkness."

Then she forgot the order of things and how they worked. She couldn't remember how to arrange the plates and glasses on the table, or how to switch off the light when she left the room (she climbed on to a chair and tried to unscrew the bulb).

She wore tattered skirts and darned stockings, which she refused to part with: "You must have a packet, the way you throw everything away!" The only feelings she could experience were anger and suspicion. In every word she detected a threat against herself. She was plagued by urgent necessities, such as buying lacquer for her hair, knowing what day the doctor would come and how much money she had in her savings book. Sometimes she affected a playful attitude, chuckling to herself to show that she was all right.

She no longer understood what she read. She paced from one room to the next, searching all the time. She emptied the contents of her wardrobe on to the bed and rearranged her dresses and mementos on different shelves. The next day she started all over again, as if she couldn't get the order right. One Saturday afternoon in January, she crammed half her clothes into plastic bags and sewed the edges together with cotton thread. When she wasn't tidying up, she would be sitting in the living room, her arms crossed, staring straight ahead of her. Nothing could make her happy.

She forgot people's names. She called me "Madame" in icy tones. She no longer recognized her own grandsons. At mealtimes, she asked them whether they got decent wages. She imagined she lived and worked on a farm where they too were employed. And yet she could see herself clearly. She felt ashamed when she soiled her nightdress, hiding it under her pillow and confessing to me one morning: "I couldn't help it." She was desperate to cling on to the world. She started to sew furiously, forming piles of scarves and handkerchiefs and joining them together with large, irregular stitches. She became attached to things, like her sponge bag which she carried around with her, entering a state of near panic as soon as she lost sight of it.

During this period, I was responsible for two road accidents. My stomach ached and I had trouble swallowing. I lost my temper and felt like crying for the slightest little thing. Sometimes the boys and I would roar with laughter, pretending to see my mother's lapses of memory as a deliberate joke on her part. I talked about her to people who didn't know her. They stared at me in silence. I felt I was going mad too. One day I drove aimlessly along country lanes for hours and hours, returning home after dusk. I started an affair with a man who repelled me.

I didn't want her to become a little girl again, somehow she didn't have the "right."

She started talking to people who weren't there. The first time it happened, I was marking some essays. I put my hands over my ears. I thought, "It's all over." Then I wrote down "Mummy's talking to herself" on a piece of paper. (I wrote those words for myself, to make the thought more bearable. Now I am writing the same words, but for other people, so that they can understand.)

She decided not to get up in the morning. She would eat only sweet things and dairy products. Anything else made her sick. Towards the end of February, the doctor had her moved to the hospital at Pontoise, where she was admitted to the gastroenterology unit. Her health improved within a few days. The nurses had to tie her to her chair because she kept trying to escape from the ward. For the first time I rinsed her false teeth, cleaned her fingernails, and applied cold cream to her face.

Two weeks later, she was moved to the geriatric unit, a modern, three-story building which stands in a small cluster of trees behind the hospital. Most of the patients there are women. Those admitted for only short visits are sent to the first floor. The second and third floors receive the old people who are entitled to stay there until they die. The top floor seems to be reserved for the disabled and the mentally handicapped. The rooms—single or double—are light and clean. They are decorated with flowered wallpaper, engravings, a wall clock, a couple of armchairs in imitation leather, and each has a small bathroom with a lavatory. Some long-term patients have to wait for months before they can get a bed, especially if there haven't been many deaths during the previous winter. My mother was sent to the first floor.

She talked animatedly and recalled scenes she thought she had witnessed the day before, a holdup or a child drowning. She told me that she had just been out shopping and that the streets were swarming with people. Fear and resentment had returned to torment her. She felt indignant at having to work her fingers to the bone for employers who didn't pay her. She was approached by men. She greeted me angrily: "I've been so hard up lately, can't even afford a piece of cheese." In her pockets she kept bits of bread left over from lunch.

Even in her condition, she refused to give in. The religious streak in her faded, she had no incentive to go to church or to keep her rosary. She wanted to get better—"They're bound to find out what the matter is"—and leave the hospital—"I'll be all right once I'm with you." She wandered from one corridor to the next until she was exhausted. She begged for wine.

One evening in April, she was already asleep at half past six, lying across the rumpled sheets in her slip. Her knees were up, showing her private parts. It was very warm in the room. I started to cry because she was my mother, the same woman I had known in my childhood. Her chest was covered in tiny blue veins.

Her statutory eight-week stay in the ward ended. She was transferred to a private nursing home, but only temporarily, because they didn't take in "confused" people. At the end of May, she was moved back to the geriatric unit at Pontoise hospital. A bed had become free on the third floor.

As she gets out of the car and walks through the

entrance, this is the last time that, despite her distracted air, she is unmistakably herself: wearing her glasses, her grey *chiné* suit, a pair of smart shoes, and stockings, her head held high. In her suitcase there are her blouses, her own underwear, and a few photographs and mementos.

She slowly slipped into a world without seasons, warm, gentle, and sweet-smelling, where there was no notion of time, just the inevitable routine of eating and going to bed. In between meals, there was nothing for her to do except walk along the corridors, stare blankly at the American soap operas and the glossy commercials on television, and sit down for dinner an hour before the food was ready, folding and unfolding her napkin feverishly. There were, I'm sure, the small parties: the free cakes handed round by charitable ladies on Thursday afternoons, a glass of champagne on New Year's Day, and the traditional sprig of lily of the valley on May Day. There was love, too, with the women still holding hands, touching each other's hair, and fighting. And, of course, the unchanging philosophy of the nurses: "Go on, Mrs. D—, have a sweet, it'll give you something to do."

Within a few weeks, she lost her self-respect. Her body began to sag and she walked around with her shoulders hunched and her head bent. She lost her glasses and her eyes took on a glazed expression. Her face looked bare, and slightly swollen, because of the tranquilizers. There was something wild about her appearance.

One by one she mislaid all her possessions, her favorite cardigan, her second pair of spectacles, and her sponge bag.

She didn't care, she had given up trying to find things. She couldn't remember what belonged to her, suddenly she had nothing of her own. One day she glanced at the Savoyard chimney sweep she had carried around with her since Annecy and remarked: "I used to have one like that." For reasons of convenience, my mother, like most of the other women, wore a smock open at the back and a flowered blouse on top. Nothing seemed to shame her now, not even wearing an incontinence pad or eating voraciously with her fingers.

She gradually found it harder to distinguish between the people around her. The words that reached her were meaningless but she replied at random just the same. She still felt the need to communicate. Her speech mechanism had remained intact, producing logical sentences and correctly pronounced words, but what she said was dictated by her imagination and bore no relation to reality. She invented the life she could no longer live: she went to Paris, she had bought herself a goldfish, she had been taken to see her husband's grave, and so on. And yet sometimes she knew: "I'm afraid my condition is irreversible." Or else she remembered: "I did everything I could to make my daughter happy and she wasn't any happier for it."

She lived through the summer—like the other residents, she was dressed in a straw hat every time she went down to sit in the gardens—and the following winter. On New Year's Day, she was given a skirt and a blouse of her own, and poured a glass of champagne. She walked more slowly now, one hand gripping the rail that ran along the walls of the corridor. Sometimes she fell down. She lost the bottom half of her false teeth and, a little later, the top half. Her lips shriveled and the lower part of her face developed into one large chin. Every time I went to see her, I was terrified she would look even less "human." When I was away from her, I pictured her with the expression and the features she'd had before, and never with those of the woman she had become.

The following summer she fractured her hipbone. They decided not to operate. There was no point in fixing her up with an artificial hip, nor, for that matter, making her new teeth and spectacles. Now she never left her wheelchair, to which she was tied by a cotton strip, wrapped firmly around her waist. She was installed in the dining room with the other women, opposite the television set.

The people who had known her wrote to me saying, "She deserved better than that." They felt that the sooner she was "out of her misery," the better. Maybe one day the whole of society will agree with them. They didn't come to see her, for them she was already dead. And yet she still wanted to live. She kept straining to get up, pressing on her good leg and tearing at the cotton strip. She tried to grab everything within her reach. She was always hungry, all her energy had become concentrated around her mouth. She liked being kissed and would purse her lips in an attempt at mimicry. She was a little girl who would never grow up.

I brought her chocolates and pastries, which I cut up into little pieces and fed to her. At first I always got the wrong sort of cake—it was either too firm or too creamy—and she couldn't eat it (the indescribable pain of seeing her struggle with the crumbs, using her tongue and her fingers to finish them up). I washed her hands, shaved her face, and sprinkled her with perfume. One day I started to brush her hair and when I stopped she said: "I like it when you do my hair." After that I brushed her hair every time I went to see her. I remained in her room, sitting opposite her. She often grabbed my skirt, passing her fingers over the fabric as if to inspect the quality. She tore up the paper from the cake shop with violence, her teeth clenched firmly together. She talked about money and former customers, laughing, her head thrown back. These were gestures she had always had, and words that had been with her all her life. I didn't want her to die.

I needed to feed her, to touch her, and to hear her.

On several occasions I felt the sudden urge to take her away and give up everything else just to look after her. I realized instantly that I was incapable of doing such a thing. (I still felt guilty about having put her into a home, even if, as people said, I "had no alternative.")

She lived through another winter. The Sunday after Easter, I went to see her with some forsythia. It was a grey, cold day. She was in the dining room with the other women. The television was on. She smiled at me as I approached. I wheeled her back into her room. I arranged the forsythia branches in a vase. I sat down beside her and gave her some chocolate to eat. She had been dressed in brown woolen socks that reached above her knees and a short smock that revealed her emaciated thighs. I washed her mouth and her hands. Her skin was warm. At one point, she grabbed at the flowers in the vase. Later on, I wheeled her back into the dining room. The television was showing *L'Ecole des*

---

† A Sunday afternoon program in which children are invited to the studio to imitate their favorite singer.

Fans.[†] I kissed her goodbye and took the lift down to the ground floor. She died the next day.

The following week, I kept remembering that Sunday, when she was alive, the brown socks, the forsythia, her mannerisms, her smile when I said goodbye, and then the Monday, when she was dead, lying in her bed. I couldn't put the two days together.

Now everything is one.

It's the end of February. The weather has turned mild and it often rains. Tonight, after I had done the shopping, I returned to the old people's home. Seen from the car park, the building looked lighter, almost welcoming. There was a light on in what used to be my mother's room. I was astonished to realize for the first time: "Someone else has taken her place." It also occurred to me that one day in the twenty-first century, I would be one of the women who sit waiting for their dinner, folding and unfolding their napkins, here or somewhere else.

Throughout the ten months I was writing this book, I dreamed of her almost every night. Once I was lying in the middle of a stream, caught between two currents. From my loins, smooth again like a young girl's, from between my thighs, long tapering plants floated limply. The body they came from was not only mine, it was also my mother's.

Every now and then, I seem to be back in the days when she was still living at home, before she left for the hospital. Although I realize she is dead, sometimes, for a split second, I expect to see her come downstairs and settle in the living room with her sewing basket. This feeling—which puts my mother's illusory presence before her real absence—is no doubt the first stage of healing.

I have just reread the first pages of this book. I was

amazed to discover that I had already forgotten some of the details, like the assistant from the morgue talking on the phone while we were waiting, or the supermarket wall smeared with tar.

A few weeks ago, one of my aunts told me that when my mother and father started going out together, they would arrange to meet in the lavatories at the rope factory. Now that my mother is dead, I wouldn't want to learn anything about her that I hadn't known when she was alive.

I see her more and more the way I imagine I saw her in my early childhood: as a large, white shadow floating above me.

She died eight days before Simone de Beauvoir.

She preferred giving to everybody, rather than taking from thèm. Isn't writing also a way of giving?

Naturally, this isn't a biography, neither is it a novel,

maybe a cross between literature, sociology, and history. It was only when my mother—born in an oppressed world from which she wanted to escape—became history that I started to feel less alone and out of place in a world ruled by words and ideas, the world where she had wanted me to live.

I shall never hear the sound of her voice again. It was her voice, together with her words, her hands, and her way of moving and laughing, which linked the woman I am to the child I once was. The last bond between me and the world I come from has been severed.

Sunday 20 April 1986 – 26 February 1987

A SEVEN STORIES PRESS
READING GROUP GUIDE

A Woman's Story
By Annie Ernaux

The following questions are suggested to enhance indi-
vidual reading and invite group discussion regarding
Annie Ernaux's *A Woman's Story*. We hope these questions provide additional topics for consideration and
generate a stimulating dialogue with others.

For a complete listing of Seven Stories Press books fea-
turing Reading Group Guides, please visit our website,
www.sevenstories.com.

DISCUSSION QUESTIONS

1. Why do you think Ernaux chooses to title her book "A Woman's Story"? To whom do you think it refers and why? What would you have chosen to title it?

2. Examine the quote from Hegel prefacing the book. What do you think he means by this? To what extent do you agree or disagree? How does this idea relate to the rest of the book?

3. Ernaux attempts to view her mother's story in a purely objective context in order "to capture the real woman, the one who existed independently from me . . ." (12) What techniques does she use stylistically to accomplish this? Do you think she is ultimately able to achieve her goal? Why or why not?

4. After her mother's funeral, Ernaux writes, "Everything was definitely over." (8) What is over? What now begins? Similarly, what does Ernaux mean when she writes, "Now everything is one"? (87)

5. Ernaux says she writes "as if there existed only one immutable order which would convey the truth about my mother (although what this truth involves I am unable to say)." (31) Plot the sequence with which Ernaux relates the events of her mother's life and death in the book. Why do you think Ernaux ultimately decides on this particular chronology? How does it connect with the larger themes of rebirth and growth? Can you find passages in the book to support your answer? And finally, in your opinion, what is the truth Ernaux wished to convey?

6. Why is Ernaux now able to "feel the power of ordinary sentences, or even clichés"? (10)

7. As Ernaux reveals the story of her mother's life, her own story is similarly bared. Compare the similarities and differences you discover between the two women in regards to their upbringing, their temperaments, their intellectual disposition, their aspirations, and their worldviews. Ernaux then predicts for herself a similar end to her mother's: "one day . . . I would be one of the women who sit waiting for their dinner, folding and unfolding their napkins, here or somewhere else." (87) Why do you think

she comes to this conclusion? Do you agree with this scenario? Why or why not?

8. Ernaux is careful to suspend judgment of her mother, of herself, and of those around her, calling herself "only the archivist." (15) What is she archiving? What moral and emotional demands does this position then place on the reader? Are there any passages you remember that particularly moved or shocked you? Would a different approach to her mother's death have ultimately been more powerful? Why or why not?

9. Ernaux writes, "I would recognize that tone of conversation between a mother and her daughter anywhere in the world." (64) What are the universal signs of a mother-daughter relationship you find throughout the book? And in your own life?

10. What are some of the idealized misconceptions children have of their parents, sometimes well past the age of childhood? Find examples in the book as well as from personal experience. How does Ernaux react when these illusions are broken?

11. Ernaux writes, "The last bond between me and the world I come from has been severed." (90) To what extent is this true? What world is she referring to? What world does she now belong to? Find passages in the book to support your answer.